PRAISE FOR

BOOK 1: THE POLARSHIELD PROJECT

"Ridley Pearson knocks it out of the park with this supersonic tale."
—**EOIN COLFER,** AUTHOR OF *ARTEMIS FOWL*

"Precocious, poignant, and powerful! I hope you packed a lunch, because you're not gonna want to put this book down."
—**JOEY BRAGG,** STAR OF *LIV AND MADDIE*

"This all-new SUPER SONS is a surefire fun read as four young strangers meet and band together against the looming backdrop of global doom."
—**DAN JURGENS,** AUTHOR OF *THE ADVENTURES OF SUPERMAN* AND *BATMAN BEYOND*

"As the breathtaking action unfolds, the mysteries pile up—and there is danger on every page. My kind of story! I want to see more, more, MORE!"
—**R.L. STINE,** AUTHOR OF *GOOSEBUMPS* AND *FEAR STREET*

SUPER

BOOK 2
THE FOXGLOVE MISSION

WRITTEN BY
Ridley Pearson

ART BY
Ile Gonzalez

Letterer: Saida Temofonte

SUPERMAN created by JERRY SIEGEL and JOE SHUSTER
SUPERBOY created by JERRY SIEGEL
By special arrangement with the JERRY SIEGEL family

MICHELE R. WELLS VP & Executive Editor, Young Reader

DIEGO LOPEZ Assistant Editor

STEVE COOK Design Director - Books

AMIE BROCKWAY-METCALF Publication Design

BOB HARRAS Senior VP - Editor-in-Chief, DC Comics

DAN DiDIO Publisher

JIM LEE Publisher & Chief Creative Officer

BOBBIE CHASE VP - New Publishing Initiatives & Talent Development

DON FALLETTI VP - Manufacturing Operations & Workflow Management

LAWRENCE GANEM VP - Talent Services

ALISON GILL Senior VP - Manufacturing & Operations

HANK KANALZ Senior VP - Publishing Strategy & Support Services

DAN MIRON VP - Publishing Operations

NICK J. NAPOLITANO VP - Manufacturing Administration & Design

NANCY SPEARS VP - Sales

SUPER SONS BOOK 2: THE FOXGLOVE MISSION

DC Comics, 2900 West Alameda Ave., Burbank, CA 91505

Printed by LSC Communications, Crawfordsville, IN, USA.

9/20/19. First Printing.

ISBN: 978-1-4012-8640-8

PEFC Certified

This product is from sustainably managed forests and controlled sources

PEFC

PEFC/29-31-337

www.pefc.org

Library of Congress Cataloging-in-Publication Data

Names: Pearson, Ridley, author. | Gonzalez, Ile, artist. | Temofonte, Saida, letterer.

Title: Super Sons : the Foxglove mission / written by Ridley Pearson ; art by Ile Gonzalez ; letterer, Saida Temofonte.

Other titles: Foxglove mission

Description: Burbank, CA : DC Zoom, [2019] | Series: Super Sons ; book 2 | Audience: Ages 8-12 | Audience: Grades 4-6 | Summary: "With their hometown in ruins, Jon and Ian are on a mission to find a sample of the deadly virus that is threatening Wyndemere and Jon's mother, Lois Lane. Meanwhile, Candace follows clues that hold the key to her destiny as she unlocks powerful abilities she never knew existed."-- Provided by publisher.

Identifiers: LCCN 2019028595 (print) | LCCN 2019028596 (ebook) | ISBN 9781401286408 (paperback) | ISBN 9781779501714 (ebook)

Subjects: LCSH: Graphic novels. | CYAC: Graphic novels. | Superheroes--Fiction. | Ability--Fiction.

Classification: LCC PZ7.7.P36 Sum 2019 (print) | LCC PZ7.7.P36 (ebook) | DDC 741.5/973--dc23

what happened in book 1?

In ***Super Sons: The PolarShield Project* (Book 1)** we learn that the country of Coleumbria is in trouble. Climate disruption is flooding major cities like Metropolis. People are moving to cities like Wyndemere where it is safer.

Jon Kent is the son of Superman and Lois Lane. He meets a girl named Tilly at school. She wonders why Jon is so interested in Superman. Jon tells her that Superman has been sent to Mars to collect special dust for the PolarShield Project. It's a science project made to slow Earth's warming.

Jon is having a hard time. His mother is very sick. His dad is on Mars. Jon is looked after by a neighbor. He tries hard to find a cure for his mom. In the library he meets a girl named Candace. She has a mysterious past and is on an important family mission.

Damian "Ian" Wayne is the son of the wealthy Bruce Wayne (Batman). Ian is fighting gangs to stop them from hurting people. He hopes his father will notice and ask him to be Batman's partner. Sadly, Bruce Wayne is too busy to pay much attention to Ian.

The kids discover that trouble is coming. Bad people plan to take over the PolarShield Project. It's up to Jon and Ian to save the planet!

A woman named Avryc leads the gangs that terrorize Wyndemere. She must be stopped. Jon discovers his mother is sick because she was poisoned. But by whom?

By the end of Book 1, Avryc is caught by the police. Jon may have found a way to save his mother. But there is much more to do. The four must continue their detective work to save the PolarShield Project and Lois Lane.

On to *The Foxglove Mission*...

ridley pearson

DAMIAN "IAN" WAYNE

Ian doesn't know his mother. He wants to fight by the side of his father, Batman. He has no powers, but lots of gadgets. He is a bit conceited and critical of others. At thirteen years old he is quite independent, and seems older.

BRUCE WAYNE/BATMAN

Billionaire head of Wayne Enterprises (W.E.). His company builds the walls holding back the flood waters. As Batman, he secretly knows Superman. He is worried about the spreading illness and wants to find a cure.

PATIENCE

Bruce Wayne's assistant. She also looks after Ian Wayne when Bruce travels.

THE FOUR FINGERS

Four young women representing various districts in Landis. Their mission is to either stop Candace from being crowned empress, or to convince her to be different. Candace treats others as friends. The Four Fingers do not.

TACO

Ian Wayne's small but lovable dog. Ian considers Taco his best friend.

CANDACE

Candace was born in Landis, a continent far from the nation of Coleumbria. Her mother was an empress before she died. Candace is fourteen and has been living with an aunt in Wyndemere for the past several years. She will soon have to return to Landis to be named empress, but only if she brings a special oil with her. Others want that oil as well.

LOIS LANE

Mother of Jon Kent. Wife of Clark Kent. An important reporter for the *Daily Planet*. She was working on a big story about a spreading illness before becoming very ill. She knows Bruce Wayne.

CLARK KENT/SUPERMAN

Father of Jon Kent. Husband of Lois Lane. As Superman he is escorting a space expedition to Mars to help the PolarShield Project and save the planet.

JON KENT

Twelve-year-old Jon is the son of Clark Kent (Superman) and Lois Lane (reporter for the *Daily Planet* newspaper). While he can't fly, he can jump high and run fast, and his skin is pretty tough. He's optimistic, full of energy, and a team player.

PERRY WHITE

Lois and Clark's boss and the publisher of the *Daily Planet*.

TILLY

Tilly spends much of her time reading. She's good with computers and all things mechanical. She goes to school with Jon Kent. She is a loyal friend.

JILL OLSEN

Lois Lane's assistant at the *Daily Planet*.

A Guide to the Characters and World of

SUPER SONS

MRS. KIACK

Neighbor of the Kent family. She sometimes looks after Jon Kent when his parents are too busy, or are away on business.

SIR REALE
A politician and businessman who works for G. Reed. When something illegal needs to be done, he makes it happen so that it appears G. Reed isn't involved.

AVRYC
A powerful woman who controls gang members in Coleumbria. Bad people pay her and her gangs to do criminal things.

PARA SOL
Para Sol is a good person who runs the government's PolarShield Project. She works closely with Dr. Cray Ving (who's not so good!).

DR. CRAY VING
A scientist working for G. Reed. He is involved with the government's PolarShield Project to stop global warming.

COLEUMBRIA
The world's most free democracy. A country with cities like Metropolis and Gotham and Wyndemere, as well as the capital city, the Coleumbrian Quarter. Climate disruption is flooding the country. Its citizens are moving inland to higher ground.

WYNDEMERE
A large city in the north of Coleumbria on the shores of an enormous inland lake. Many residents of coastal cities are moving to Wyndemere.

LANDIS
A vast continent across the ocean that's controlled by an evil general.

Wyndemere Shipyard.
It's now or never.
If I don't get onto that boat, I'll never solve Mother's mystery.

She's here. No matter what, Candace must **not** get on the barge.

Ian, who are those girls?
I thought **Superboy** knows everything.
They're chasing Candace. That's all that matters, **Batkid.**
I'll set off the fireworks in this crate. You help Candace.

"One distraction coming up!"

There she is! Those crates! Stop her!
Okay! Courage!
Five... four... three... two...

KA-BLAM

Huh?

Now!

Stop! Wait for me!
THUNK
THUNK
THUNK

It's too far away! I'm not going to make it!

Stop her!
Huh? Superboy?

Out of my way!
WHOMP
Oof!

Three against one?
I like these odds.

We couldn't let you try this alone!

Rat-a-tat-attack the boy!

Thank you, Jon!
I hope you can solve your mother's mystery.
Me, too!

Bashata!
Natasa, take this! Get the boy!

Batkid! Matches!
KRAK

Thanks. But I had it under control.
Of course you did.
Do you think we'll see her again?
I hope so. She's part of our team now.
Agreed! But now I wish we'd gone with her.

Do you think Candace will make it to the Coleumbrian Quarter?
It's a long way. And she's alone. I'm worried about her.
Same here.
I'm worried about my father, too.

PolarShield Project Control Center.

Dr. Sol? Coffee, two sugars?
Thank you, Dr. Ving.

Is the shield still keeping the Arctic cold?

If Superman brings us the asteroid dust, the Earth just might stand a chance!
Drink up, my dear. It's good to the last drop.

Out late again last night.
Mom won't come out of her coma without my help, Mrs. Kiack.

You're not a doctor.

No, but I'm a Super son.
No. But I'm no quitter.

A nice girl stopped by today.
Tilly?
That's weird.

"Not Tilly. Said she's a friend of someone named Candace."

So polite and pretty.
And Candace's enemy!

Wyndemere Middle School.

SUPERMAN'S MARS MISSION
Will space dust save the world?
Jon, you're obsessed.

No, Tilly, I'm interested.

I realize the Earth warmed–

DAILY PLANET
"–Metropolis flooded–

"–and PolarShield acted like an umbrella to cool the poles.
NORTH POLE
90N

"That scientists said they needed space dust–

"–and that only Superman can see the stuff as it passes Mars.

But you're *obsessed!*

If the zip line works, then I'm secure over there.

Uh-huh.

You're not even listening, Patience.

Father! It's been so long!

Just checking in. I'm safe. I wouldn't be over here if it weren't critical.

I know.

Be ready, son. I may need you.

Wyndemere Station Bridge.
That was the last working bridge.
If Avryc's thugs hadn't blown it up, following Candace would've been a lot easier.
We'll never catch her now. We don't even know where she's going!
I wouldn't be so sure about that. Those boys must know something about it. After all, they helped her escape.

North Central University.
My mom knows a doctor here. I sent him our map of where the virus is spreading.

I'm sorry to hear about your mother's illness.

We think my mom was contaminated on purpose.

That's a matter for the government's disease division.
And if they won't help?
What *is* it, exactly?

This virus isn't found in nature.
Meaning?

It was created in a lab, which means it's intended to harm people.

Like some kind of weapon?
Exactly!
Can you make an anecdote?
Antidote. We would need a much larger sample of the virus.

Then we need to find where they're making it.
Such matters are better left to the government. It's not for kids.

Us? We wouldn't try anything.

Thank you for coming. I will tell the government right away.

Hey!
LAB

I heard you back there. Look, if this virus is from the black market, there's only one possible lab making it.
Where?
Cinapolis.
Never heard of it.

The place is completely underwater. But gangs there are making illegal drugs of all kinds. And maybe, just maybe, your virus.
Is it across the Tamron River? All of the bridges are out.
Thank you, sir. Come on, Jon, we'll think of something.

Somewhere in the middle of the river...

Gah! Another vision!

Eight years ago.
Keep the floodgates open!
But, General Al'Feasnc, that'll kill thousands of people who live downstream!
And the problem is?

Drop everything!
Run for your lives!

You will pay for this! Someday! Somehow!

DAILY PLANET
You should have told me about Candace leaving before now.
We couldn't have stopped her. So, we protected her. She's following her mother's clue about some kind of cactus.
Random!

Scan these documents.
Please, Mr. White, can't we do something ***interesting?***

Wyndemere Jail.
Routine check of her restraints. Meet me at the next cell.
Yes, Sergeant.

Avryc, the boy was seen at the university speaking to a chemist.
Tell Sir Reale he must stage my escape ***soon.***

As the sun begins to set over the river.

I've seen this before!

Mother? Here? Seriously?
Check out dem birds.
Ain't seen nothin' like it.

Survivor's
float. Catch
your breath!

What the heck?

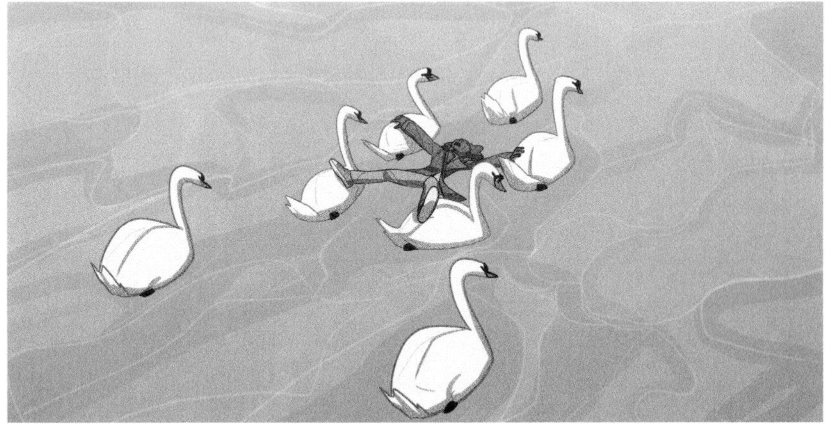

A very changed Coleumbria.

What happened to the Coleumbria I love?

Hi, I'm Tori. Are you injured?
Shocked. Stunned. But I'm okay. Thanks.
I'm going to the Coleumbrian Quarter.
It's dangerous. Robbers. Thieves. You should stay here tonight.

You're a doctor?
No. I deliver medicines to places like this.
Medicines?
They're scarce. What I do is not exactly legal. But these people need medicine.
Have you been to the Coleumbrian Quarter?
Not for a while. I can take you partway. It's safer traveling together.
Thank you so much.
Do you have family there?

Meow!

Thank goodness. We made it.
I'm calling a council meeting.

Mother? Why the secret meeting?

General Al'Feasnc did this. I swear on all that's good and right to bring his rule to an end.
No matter what it takes!

All in favor?
Aye!

How many times are you going to look at that?
I miss him.

Be ready, son. I may need you.

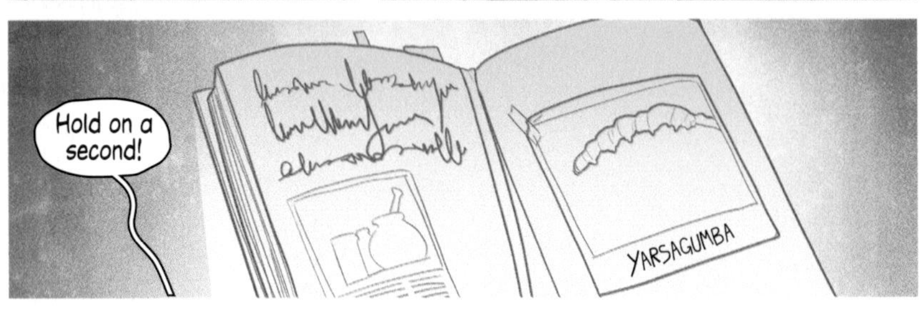
Hold on a second!
YARSAGUMBA

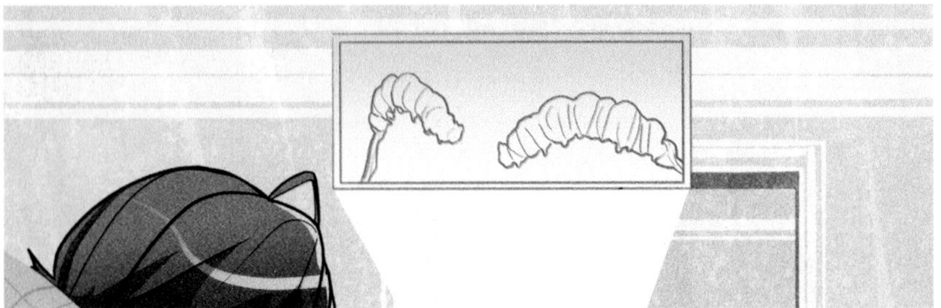

There's this stuff that grows *inside* caterpillars in Nepal.
It's a rare, powerful medicine!
Father's looking for a cure for the contamination!
We don't know that, Ian.
"Father visited Jon's mother in the hospital before he left, right?"
"Yes. They were investigating PolarShield together."

What?
So maybe **that's** why they poisoned her!

DING DONG
Jon! There she is! That girl who came looking for you the other day.

Not good!
Listen carefully. I need you to hold on to me.

And I need you to stay calm.

Ah...okay. I guess.

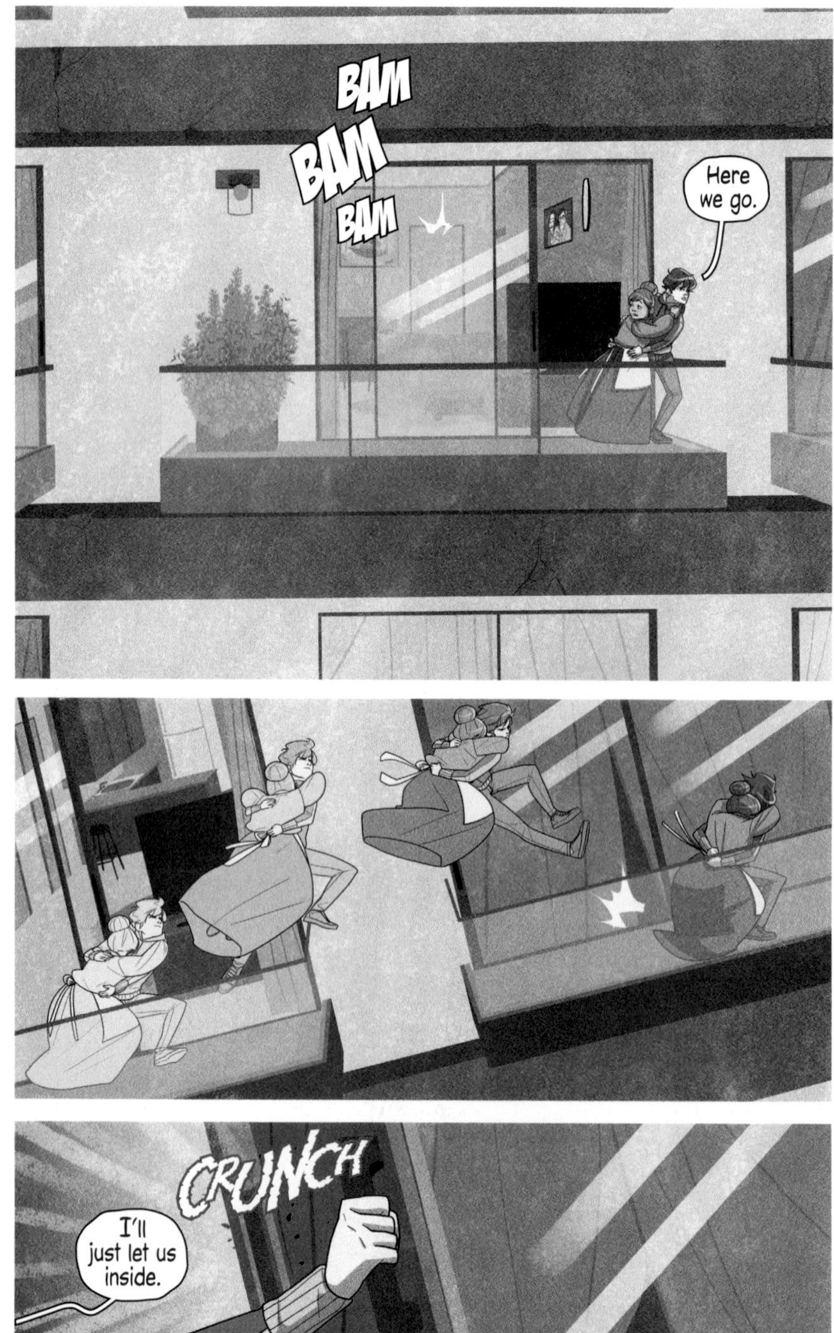
BAM
BAM
BAM
Here we go.
CRUNCH
I'll just let us inside.

Two people do not just vanish!
I swear they were here. I saw them enter the building.
Do not waste my time ever again, Natasa!

BEEP
BEEP

Thanks for the heads-up, Jon. I'll watch for those girls!

PANIC
BUTTON

BEEP
BEEP

Ian, I'm going in now!
Keep it locked. Use the Bat-Phone!

Time to suit up.
Gotcha!
Patience, stay put. Stay safe.
Be careful!

YAP!
YAP!
Where has she gone?

YAP!
YAP!

Take that!

FIRE EQUIPMENT
You have until the count of three before I wash you down these stairs. Now go!

Candace, it's time you told me about the birds.

You are a long way from home.
I am from a family line in Upper Landis.
Coleumbria has been my home since I was a child.

My grandmother always had birds nearby. I never thought much of it.

"It seemed perfectly normal to me."

"I'd forgotten all about it until... recently. Now they follow me.
"They **help** me. I don't know what's happening."
You are so lucky, child. Birds represent freedom—the gift of song and one's voice being heard. This could be a gift passed down to you.
I just thought it was something **odd.**
Maybe there's a message you're to bring to others. What if it's not something **odd,** but something powerful? What if that power lies within you, waiting to take flight?
From here my friend Jacob will guide you. Trust him. I will miss you, Candace.
Thank you for everything!

Back in Wyndemere.
PAWN SHOP
CLOSED

From this angle I think I can see...

Tilly!

TAP TAP

ZODIAC
GO!
WYNDEMERE
Could I sleep here on your floor? Just for tonight?
Sure. Of course! As long as you need.
TILLY

Tamron River Bridge.

Aminia, are you sure about this?
It's going to work, Khalifa.

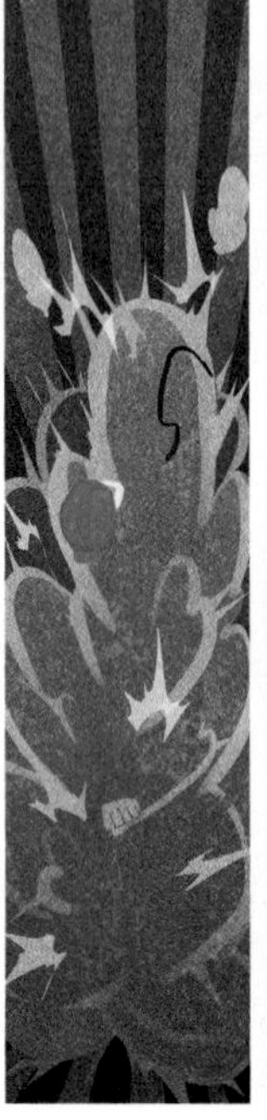

Act natural. We are just four workers.
Easy for you to say. My zipper's stuck!

"The boys are dead ends. It's time to look elsewhere for aid in capturing Candace.
"And I know just the place..."

The Daily Planet.

This is so boring.
Boring would be ***better*** than this. Ian has got to get us across the river to Cinapolis.

Chief! Come see this!

The video purports to show four unidentified young women illegally crossing the Tamron River.
Those are the same four girls who attacked Ian and me.
That can't be coincidence.
They know about Cinapolis!
Candace is in danger, Jon!
We're all in danger if ***they*** get the virus.
Call Ian. Tell him it's now or never.

This is awful. We should help them.

Get real, Bashata! They're hopeless. We help ourselves, starting with that canoe!

No one is helpless! Not ever!

Shut up and follow orders.

Not going to happen.

We need the canoe for the bridge work.

We'll return it with the shift change.

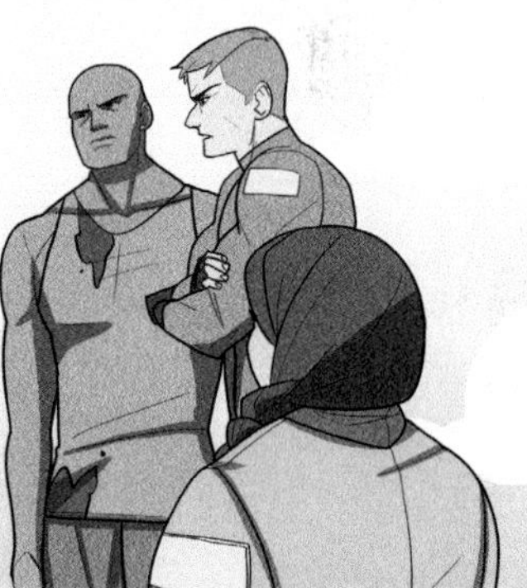

I've heard nothing about this. Why should we trust you?
If *you* want to fix the bridge, you can take my place.

Let them do their work!

Come back here!
Liars!
You'll regret this! There's nothing for a thousand miles!

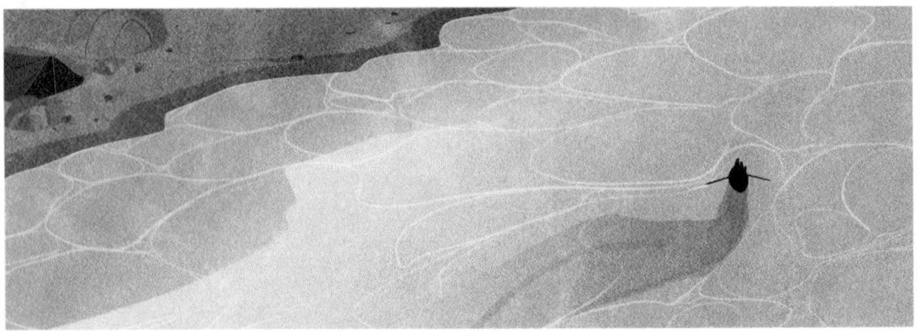

The Coleumbrian Woods.

Why sleep in a tree, Jacob?

It's safer for us. For you.

What's with the owls?

That's not terribly comforting.

You're too close. Move away from me!

Tori didn't tell you about the reward being offered for Bird Girl, did she?
Reward? Are you serious?
Never been more serious in my life.

Cinapolis, Freeland East.
Three days later.
What is that place?
It's flooded, that's what. Abandoned.
I wouldn't be so sure.

We should never have come here.

State your business in Cinapolis!

We accept no Flood Runners.

I am Aminia, Princess of Early Landis, heiress to the ruler of the birthland of Ja, governor of Gree. I wish to speak to your gatekeeper.

Demand to speak to your gatekeeper, if you must know.

We're in a bit of a hurry, if you don't mind.

I've heard you run the black market.
She is an entrepreneur.

And you are?
An entrepreneur's friend and associate.

You wish to trade? To barter?

"The migration from the flooded cities is from the east to the west.
"We seek news of a girl—the Bird Girl—who travels **west** to **east.**"
Your offer?
Your boatman will tell you of our powers. We offer to not use our powers **against you.**
You dare threaten Sinba?
Oh, yes. You will find the Bird Girl or you will become nothing but a memory in this city.

How dare you—!
One condition: You will use these powers to persuade certain prisoners to talk.
What? No way!
Agreed. Believe me, it will be *our pleasure.*

This auto drive will take us to the bridge. See if there's a way across.
It's a security zone. We won't get in.
Once this is on the windshield we will.
I feel like I'm being selfish, trying to get the virus in order to help my mother.
30% OFF!
We are being good sons. Super sons.
What about being good friends?
Life is complicated. We need a plan.

I have one! As much as I don't like it, you and I need to work together.
TAP TAP
You really **are** a dreamer, Jon Kent.

I'm Ian Wayne. Bruce's son. I'm here to inspect the steel shipment.
Very well, Mr. Wayne.

Patience also told me what to say.

We're cooked. There's no way across.
Oh ye of little faith!

The Coleumbrian Woods.
We'll be there soon.
Good! My feet are killing me.

CRACK
Hide!

Where, exactly?
I could use a little help here!

Where's the girl?
PWUM

She went north with the medic.

The next lie will be your last.

Where.
Is the.
Bird.
Girl?

Here she is!

Attack!

CAW
CAW
CAW

News of this will travel fast.
Just like in middle school!
I wish my friends were here.

Wake up! Ian wants us.

With my super-vision I see a bunch of computers inside, and at least one person.
You amaze me.

Welcome! Come up!

I have a plan to cross the river.
I knew you could do it!
We go in full costume.
All of us!

Smallville.
Many years ago.

And many years
after that.

Cinapolis. Now.
"I wish to collect the reward for reporting the Bird Girl.

She travels to the Armorac Split and the Flood Runner raft dock there.

I sense he has more to tell.
I swear, that is all!

Aminia, please ensure the prisoner speaks the truth.
Prisoner?! What about the reward?
My pleasure.

Noooo!
Please, please, I told you *everything.*
We will know soon enough.

Back in Wyndemere.
You know how they shut off city power at midnight because it's mostly solar?
Yeah? So?
So, my plan is for you and Tilly to create a diversion for me, and then I'll create one for you two.

Yoo-hoo?

Huh?
What?

Puppet Girl is ready for action!

Whoa. Nice costume!
Now to prep for the plan.

"I'm going to zip-line the power lines."

Are you crazy?
You'll be electrocuted.

Not after midnight I won't. The city power will be turned off.
But no one must see me—us—which is why we need the diversions.

Later.

So I just run around the security building to sound the alarm?
They'll chase you. They won't look up at the wires. Ian will get across.
If they catch up to you, then you jump, just like we planned.

You seem so sad.
I don't like being left behind.
There's stuff to do here. Besides, you'll sleep better without a smelly boy on your floor.

Yeah, so true!
That's why I'm sad.

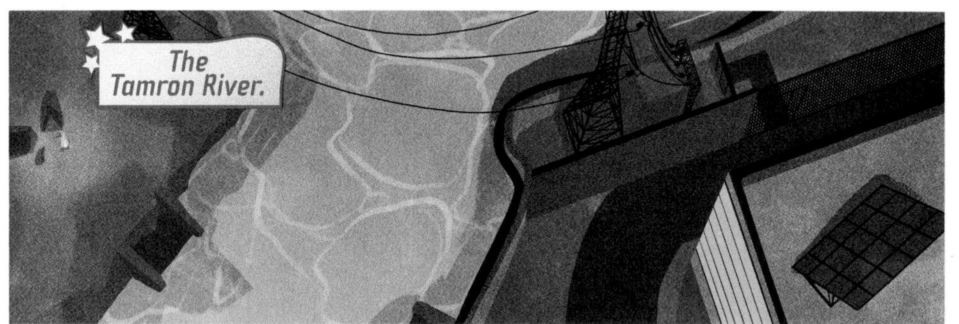
The Tamron River.

12:00

"Ready for your move."

Just as we practiced. Give me a two-minute head start.
I'm good.
Good and terrified.

BLEET
Intruder detected! Halt, or you will be apprehended!
Come and get me!
I hope the power's still off.

Halt!

This had better work. One small leap for Jon, one giant leap for humankind.

It's him!

BBB...MMM...BBB...MMM

Sorry, **partner,** but I'm going alone.

You two have fun over there.

Why would he do this?
Ian's all about the glory.
You have to get over there, Superboy. Who knows how dangerous getting the virus sample will be!
I wish for once I didn't agree with you.
If they see you, they'll turn the power on and fry you.
Yeah, I think this requires a ***leap of faith.***

It's way too far, Jon.
If I don't go now, I'll never catch him.
Don't look down.
WHOOSH

I bet I can be tracked with this. Maybe this metal will block the frequency.

MILITARY

QUACK
QUACK

Where'd you come from?

Stop it! What the heck are you doing?

You are *not* pointing down that path. That is *not* possible!

Ouch! Okay! Okay!

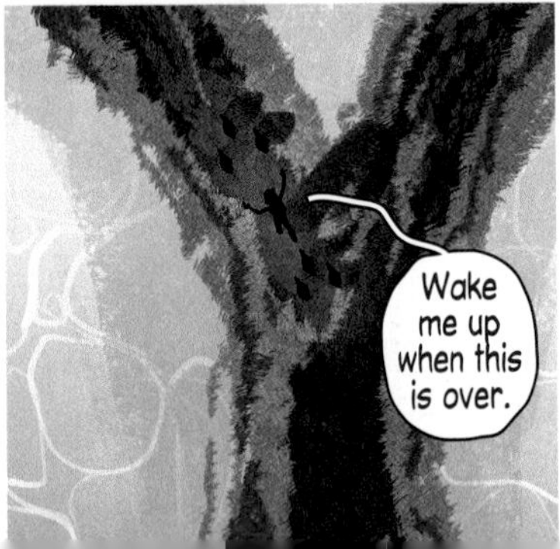
Wake me up when this is over.

I must be totally out of my mind to follow a bunch of birds.

No way!

It's him!
Ducks and cover! Sneak attack mode!

You betrayed me!

Huh?

It's always about you, isn't it, Batkid?

How about your friends?
Who else can I trust?
Break out the violins!
From here, we go on together. No secrets.

No can do, Superboy. If I need you, I'll call.

If you need me, it'll be too late to call.
You're too...**nice** for me, Superboy. I work differently.

Your father doesn't.
Leave him out of this.
Why are we doing any of this?
What would Bruce Wayne think about how you treat your friends?
I said **shut up!**

Oof!
WHOM MP

SLAM

Huh?

WHACK

Ow! We've got company!

Oof!
Hear me sing: Take wing and sting.
Jump me out of here.
Do I hear a please?
Shut up! Do it! Now!
Ouch!
Ahh!
Jump!
Oww!

Welcome to Cinapolis.

Let's lock them up and prepare to travel to the Armorac Split. The prisoner was telling the truth. Candace is heading there.

Good to see you, Patience! I'm closing in on obtaining a possible counteragent.

The hidden tracking device in his new costume is working well. That was a brilliant idea!
Ian has taken a big risk crossing the Tamron River alone.
Should I alert the Eastern Coleumbrian authorities?

I think not. Other options?
Tilly's gone silent. You could pressure **Mr. Mylark** about the contamination at Sage Foods. My guess is he knows where Ian's heading.
Consider it done!

In business news, Dr. Cray Ving will become the new director of PolarShield following the unexpected death of Dr. Para Sol.
A private company, PolarShield is currently the most important climate stabilization program in the world.
CNH

Defend the Planet
POLARSHIELD
Congratulations, Doctor.

Your plan is working, sir. I run PolarShield now.
There are questions being asked that we can ill afford to have answered. Do you understand what I'm telling you?
Yes, sir. I'll take care of it. Those voices will be silenced.
Make it quick. We haven't done all this work for nothing.

Finally! The Split!

Options?
Outnumbered. Trapped.
I have one protective animal: my birds. They have four: rodents, reptiles, insects, and cats.
Odds of victory? Quickly, Candace, quickly!

Consider your options. You're alone.
A mind reader, too?
You can't win.
Yet I never lose.
Joining us is not losing.
Join *you?* I've learned more about who I am now.
I am Candace, Empress-in-Waiting of Upper Landis...
River Queen, patron of all feathered things, and Guardian of Gree.
You have pledged to obey the line of Candace.
You have two options: Kill me or join me.

To kill me will curse you and your people for generations to come. Your decision.
We see a Landis unified by strength. Five Fingers of the Foxglove, a single hand.

A powerful hand. An unrelenting hand.

There, we differ. Again, you are faced with a choice.

I'm afraid we lack full control of our vestiges. Once you are crowned, that will change.
So be it.
That's a weak excuse if I've ever heard one.

You underestimate me. You disrespect me!

This isn't over!

Cinapolis.

You okay?
They stuck me in the leg with a ginormous needle!
Baby!
Shut up!

They left my costume but took my Batbelt. I need it back.

Wait a second! They took our wristbands! If the goons unwrap our wristbands, then we can be tracked! Patience will try to bring us home.
Not until we get the virus. Not until we find Candace.
Exactly!

Wyndemere.

Isn't that Mr. Wayne's secretary?
CHEWS
CHEWS
CHEWS

Ian's transmitter!

Mr. Wayne? Ian's in Cinapolis! I thought the city had been abandoned.
That's interesting...

He's not answering, and he's not moving. I'm so worried!
Don't worry, I'm on it!

Welcome to the Coleumbrian Quarter.

Yes. Thank you. It's amazing.

Without a pass, you're allowed a two-day visit. Don't be here after that or, if you are, don't get caught. They send you to Flood Runner townships. It isn't pretty.

Two days. Got it. Thanks!

So where do I start?

Wait! What? Ian's wristband! Jon!
BEEP BEEP

He **is** in Cinapolis! I need a plan!

North Central University.

I need a favor. I need you to hold someone's attention. You're the only person I could think to ask.

I need my Batbelt. It has all my *tricks.*
You're strong enough to bust down the door, dude. So get to it.

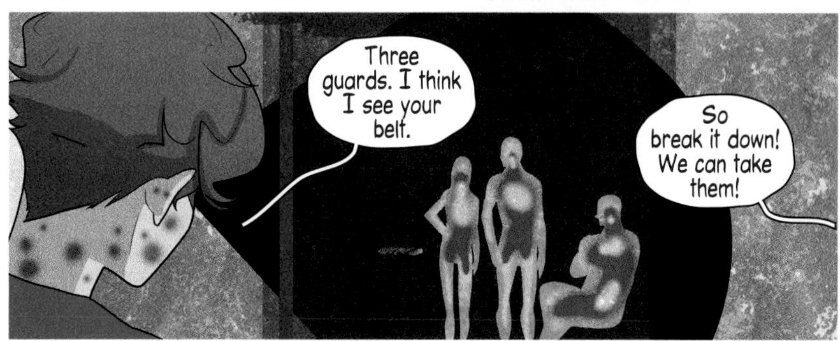
Three guards. I think I see your belt.
So break it down! We can take them!

No, we need a plan.
That is a plan. What more do you need?

This is how we're going to do it. Watch carefully.

Ready or not, here we come.

Columbia
National Garden

Penstemon
Pinifolius
Luminous

DESERT
LANDS

I think I've found it. My mother's clue. I can feel it here!

Desert Lands is closing in *ten* minutes. Please use the east doors.

Desert Lands is closing in *five* minutes.

The **anointing oil!** This is what you were leading me to, Mother! The key to the throne of Landis!

Look, Mom!

Are those all birds?

Have you ever seen anything like that?

I thought you should know that Ian Wayne asked for my department's help with a contagious virus.

What? When?

I believe he is headed to a black market lab in *Cinapolis.*
Thank you for coming here to tell me.

Hang on, boys! I'm coming!

Set destination: Cinapolis.
Destination set: Cinapolis.
Set: manual override.
We're going to make sure no one sees us.

Dr. Ving, our friends the Fingers have the two boys. They are closing in on the girl.
Your orders?
That has proven a most worthy alliance.
If I have to tell you, you aren't paying attention.

Two guards to the left. One straight ahead. Your belt to the right.
This is going to be fun!

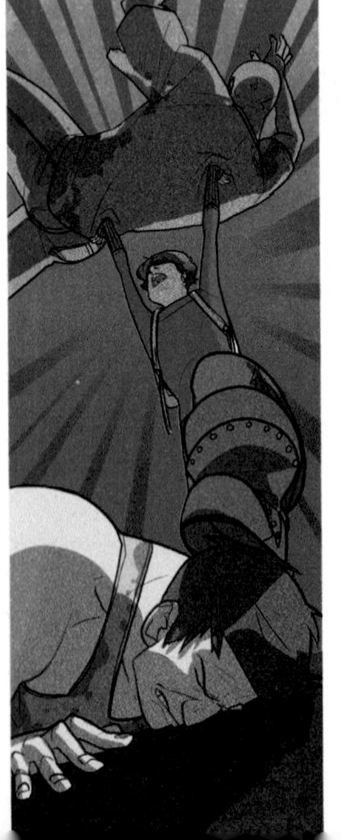

PSSST-

They escaped!

WOOSH

There! That's it! We need to destroy the virus!

What do you think is in that case?
I don't think it's candy.
We've got to burn it down, Superboy.
If we evacuate the building, we can destroy the equipment once everyone's gone...
And prevent more of the virus from being made.
I have an idea. Wristbands on.

They've escaped!
You sure this will work?
Shhh!

He mentioned the lab.
Sound the alarm! Quickly, to the lab!
Khali, grab the suitcase with the finished virus. We can't let the boys get it.

They're going to lead us right to it!

RINNNG

The water is contaminating the formula. Let's get out of here!

This bridge should give me some cover.

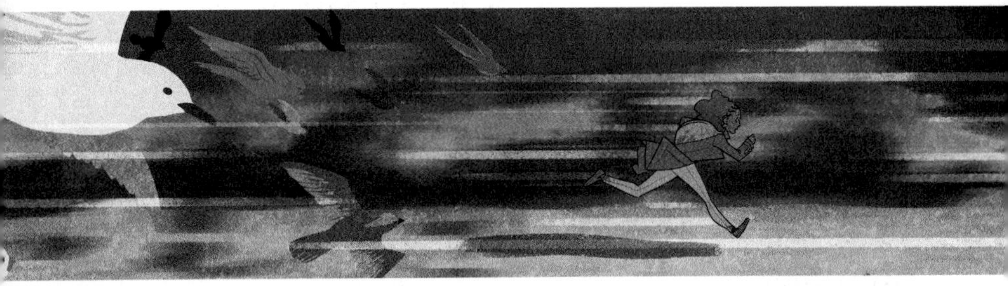

Wait a second!
Bats are **mammals,** not **birds!**

What's going on?

Columbia National Garden

Oh no! It's locked!

Don't be scared. Come willingly and we'll do you no harm.
I'm not sweating because I'm scared. It's my boiling hot skin. I wish I could **cool off!**

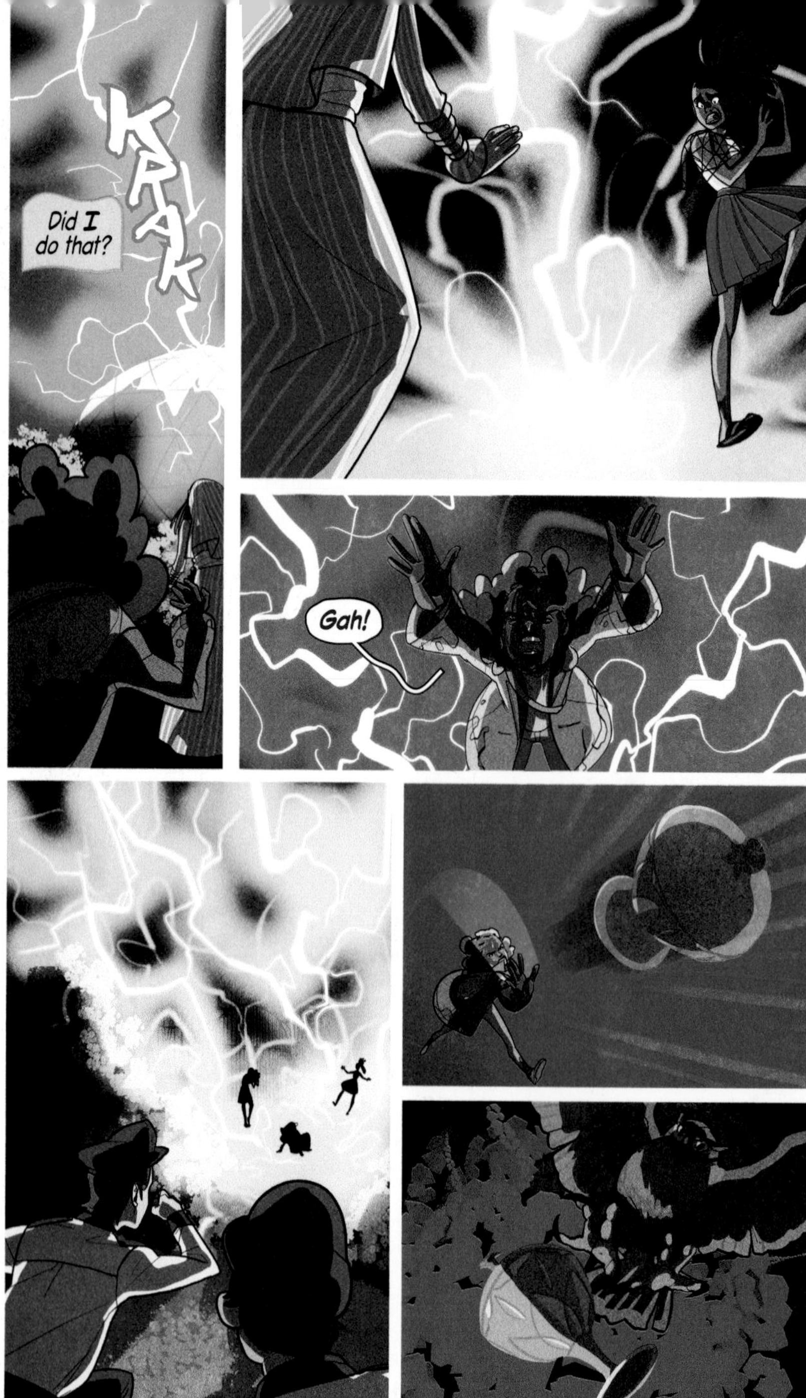
KRAK
Did I do that?
Gah!

KRAK

Where'd she go?
Vanished.

What now, Mother?

I have no idea what to actually do with this.

The next day.
Good to have you back, Khali and Natasa.

You are certain?

This little one found Candace! She's just up the canal. Let's go!

I wish... I wish the *fish*...

Take this message to warn Candace.

The lab is destroyed. Now to get to the Coleumbrian Quarter.

How will we ever find the Four Fingers?

I've got you now!

Patience to the rescue.
Yeah. Except it's Tilly!

This thing has radar, right?
The best! So?
Let's fine-tune it to look for small objects.
I don't get it.
We need to find birds. Lots of them.

What's this?

SPLOOSH

A message? Aminia is nearby!
We have her now!

My birds, I need help!

Yes—

To keep the birds from helping her!
She's ours now!

Come with us or we take the baby and leave.
No one is that cruel! Separate a mother from her baby?
You want to bet?

Back at the Daily Planet.
Mr. White, a riot has broken out in the jail holding the terrorist Avryc.
Get over there right away! Take a photographer with you.
PLANET

Look at them all!
The shipyard. That must be where Candace is.

WHOOP

TRIP

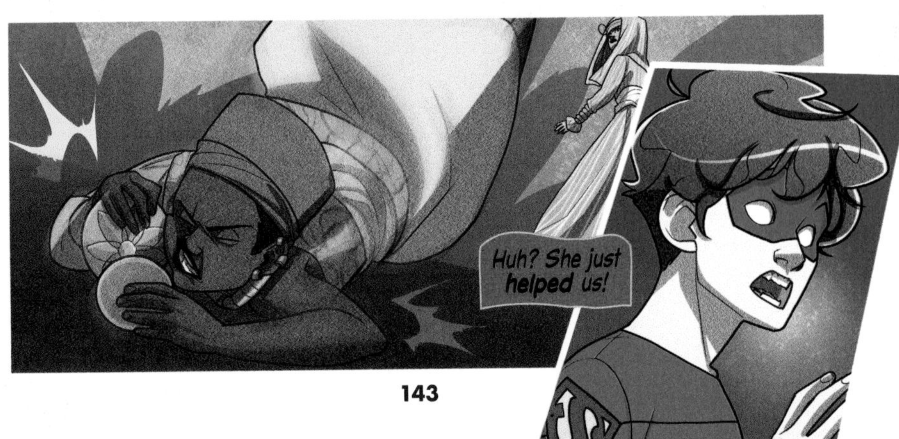
Huh? She just helped us!

Yes!
VRROOSH

That suitcase she had, they've still got the virus.
That's my mother's only hope to live!

Thanks to you all, I've got the oil and I know where they're going.

You do? Where?
Home.

Wyndemere Jail.
There she is!
Two more pulls on the rope and Avryc is free!
We've got our leader back.

They poisoned my mother.
And they wanted my mother to stop writing her story.
And the Devil's Head restaurant. They were testing the virus.
At least you got your jar back.
They have taken the poison to my land. I must stop them.
If I only knew what to do with it.
Let me see it.

The blue beads must be water—a river. The star, a location on the river.

Stars. They form a constellation.
Wait a second! I know that night sky!
It's seen from Upper Landis! Tilly, you're a genius.

We set sail for Mochi at once.
Aye-aye!

That ship is going to a place called Mochi.
Mochi? That's a port in Lower Landis!
Ready? 
As I'll ever be.

Good luck, Candace!

Wyndemere Hospital.
We're going to figure this out, Mom. We will get you a cure.
We will get you a cure.
"I promise."
To be continued in SUPER SONS BOOK 3: ESCAPE TO LANDIS!

PHOTO CREDIT: DAVID BARRY

ridley pearson is an Edgar nominee, a Fulbright Fellow, and a #1 *New York Times* bestselling author of more than 50 award-winning suspense and young adult adventure novels. His novels have been published in two dozen languages and have been adapted for both network television and the Broadway stage. Ridley's middle grade series include *Kingdom Keepers, Steel Trapp,* and *Lock and Key*. His first original graphic novel, *Super Sons: The PolarShield Project* was published in April 2019 by DC. Ridley plays bass guitar in an all-author rock band with other bestselling writers (Dave Barry, Amy Tan, Mitch Albom, Scott Turow, Greg Iles, and occasionally Stephen King). He lives and writes in the Northern Rockies along with his wife, Marcelle.

ile gonzalez illustrated her first comic strip while in kindergarten and she grew up to study fashion design in college. Deciding graphic storytelling was her first true love, she refocused her creative efforts and landed her first paid work at the digital storytelling company Madefire, working exclusively for them and co-creating their popular middle grade series *The Heroes Club*. Ile most recently illustrated *Super Sons: The PolarShield Project* from DC .

The adventure continues!

BOOK 3
ESCAPE TO LANDIS

Check out a sneak peek of
Super Sons Book 3: Escape to Landis,
coming soon from DC!

The Coleumbrian Quarter.

That night.
I hear voices over there in that window.
Your super-hearing certainly comes in handy, Superboy.

Someone's in there. We should call the police, Batkid.
We need proof it's Avryc and her gang. Let's go get some real evidence.

I think that's called irony.
FEDERAL POLICE BUZZARD'S POINT PRECINCT

Time to program this little baby to projection mode!

Holographic rats. Go get 'em, fellas!

Huh?

Oof!

One down. Let's crash this party.

We must cover our tracks now. The Landis operation has begun. Millions there will soon be sick—a wicked empire in control! Isn't it ***wonderful***?
But for that to happen, we must leave no evidence.
No witnesses. That includes those rebel boys who think they're so special!
Boss lady, Gunther isn't checking in.
Search the place.

WOMP
Get them!
WEEEOOO
She's gone! Let's get out of here!
WOOPWOOPWOOP
POLICE
I saw two guys leave and called the cops.
Good thinking, Puppet Girl! About time!
I hate that Avryc got away. ***Again***!

One hour later.
News 7 brings you live images of the Devil's Head restaurant fire. Things look out of control.
Looks like she is destroying evidence of the virus even as far away as Wyndemere.
The Four Fingers have taken the flu virus to Landis to make millions sick! Our friend Candace has left us to try to stop them. And now, Avryc is winning.
This is not good.
To be continued in SUPER SONS: ESCAPE TO LANDIS!